Mama Bunny's Good Pie

Lisa Moser

illustrated by
Sally Garland

Albert Whitman & Company
Chicago, Illinois

For the kind writers in my life who have made the
journey so sweet: Gretchen, Dori, JoAnn, Sara, Sheri,
Thelma, Kate, Ann, Lisl, Jamie, Miranda, and Linda
—LM

To Mum
—SG

Library of Congress Cataloging-in-Publication data
is on file with the publisher.
Text copyright © 2022 by Lisa Moser
Illustrations copyright © 2022 by Albert Whitman & Company
Illustrations by Sally Garland
First published in the United States of America in 2022
by Albert Whitman & Company
ISBN 978-0-8075-5224-7 (hardcover)
ISBN 978-0-8075-5225-4 (ebook)
Printed in China
10 9 8 7 6 5 4 3 2 1 WKT 26 25 24 23 22 21

Design by Rick DeMonico

For more information about Albert Whitman & Company,
visit our website at www.albertwhitman.com.

A jolly spring wind danced up Fiddlehead Hill
and tapped on the window for the little bunnies
to come out and play.

Mama Bunny rolled out piecrust and poured in a bowlful of blueberries. As her darlings waved and scattered down the hillside, she added a pinch of sugar for each of them.

One for Maple,
one for Meadow,
two for Daisy and Dew.

And one apiece for
Cabbage, Radish,
Pansy, Plum, and Lou.

She baked the pie in the oven. When she felt the jolly spring wind dance by again, she set the pie outside to cool.

Goodbye, good pie!

At the front gate, Maple jumped into the flower box
to pick all Mama's prettiest, prized flowers for her hat.

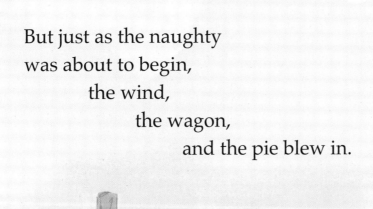

But just as the naughty
was about to begin,
the wind,
the wagon,
and the pie blew in.

"Pie!" said Maple, and she ate up a big slice.

After she was finished, Maple thought about Mama Bunny and her pie—and her kindness. And then she had a new idea.

"I shouldn't pick all of these flowers for myself. I'll do something kind instead."

She jumped up and
watered the flowers.

Then she pushed the wagon down the
hill, and the jolly wind helped it along.
   "Mama's pie has sweetened my day.
I'll share that pie. It's on the way.

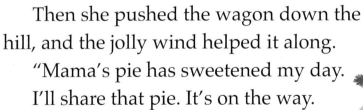

Goodbye, good pie!"

Deep in the orchard, Meadow tipped
over a barrel for a game of apple bowling.

But just as the naughty
was about to begin,
the wind,
the wagon,
and the pie blew in.

"Pie!" exclaimed Meadow, and she ate up a big slice.

After she was finished, Meadow thought about Mama Bunny and her pie—and her kindness. And then she had a new idea.

"I shouldn't ruin all of these good apples. I'll do something kind instead."

Then she gathered up all the apples, picked a few more, and put them all back in the barrel.

She pushed the wagon down the hill, and the jolly wind helped it along.
  "Mama's pie has sweetened my day.
I'll share that pie. It's on the way.

Goodbye, good pie!"

Back by the clothesline, Daisy and Dew pulled down two clean socks, for sack races.

But just as the naughty
was about to begin,
the wind,
the wagon,
and the pie blew in.

"Pie!" cheered Daisy and Dew, and they ate up two big slices. After they were finished, Daisy and Dew thought about Mama Bunny and her pie—and her kindness. And then they had a new idea.

"We shouldn't muddy up all of this clean laundry. We'll do something kind instead."

They hung the socks back on the clothesline and sorted the clothespins for good measure.

Then they pushed the wagon down the hill, and the jolly wind helped it along.
"Mama's pie has sweetened our day. We'll share that pie. It's on the way.

Goodbye, good pie!"

In the garden, Cabbage and Radish started to
pull up all the stakes to make a raft.

But just as the naughty
was about to begin,
the wind,
the wagon,
and the pie blew in.

"Pie!" hollered Cabbage and Radish, and they ate up two big slices.
After they were finished, Cabbage and Radish thought about Mama
Bunny and her pie—and her kindness. And then they had a new idea.
"We shouldn't wreck the garden. We'll do something kind instead."

They straightened all the stakes and weeded the garden rows.

Then they pushed the wagon down the hill, and the jolly wind helped it along. "Mama's pie has sweetened our day. We'll share that pie. It's on the way.

Goodbye, good pie!"

Over by the pump, Pansy and Plum filled an empty can with water and waited to splash Lou when he hopped by.

But just as the naughty
was about to begin,
the wind,
the wagon,
and the pie blew in.

"Pie!" called Pansy and Plum, sharing the pie with Lou. They ate up three big slices.

After they were finished, Lou thought about butterflies. But Pansy and Plum thought about Mama Bunny and her pie—and her kindness. And then they had a new idea.

"We shouldn't pick on each other. We'll do something kind instead."

They poured the water onto a strawberry patch instead of onto Lou. And they all gave each other strawberries and a hug.

Then they pushed the wagon down the hill, and the jolly wind helped it along. "Mama's pie has sweetened our day. We'll share that pie. It's on the way.

Goodbye, good pie!"

Mama Bunny headed down the hill, gathering her darlings for a picnic. The little bunnies ran and played with the jolly spring wind.

Then they piled into the wagon, and
Mama Bunny pulled them home.

Back at home, Mama Bunny tucked them into bed and gave them each a kiss.

One for Maple,

one for Meadow,

two for Daisy
and Dew.

And one apiece for
Cabbage, Radish,
Pansy, Plum, and Lou.

Mama Bunny sat on her
front stoop to watch the first
stars twinkle into the sky.

And just as her day
was about to end,
the wind,
the wagon,
and the pie blew in.

"Goodbye, good pie."